The Day of the Dog

George Barr McCutcheon

THE DAY OF THE DOG

BY

George Barr McCutcheon

I'll catch the first train back this evening, Graves. Wouldn't go down there if it were not absolutely necessary; but I have just heard that Mrs. Delancy is to leave for New York to-night, and if I don't see her to-day there will be a pack of troublesome complications. Tell Mrs. Graves she can count me in on the box party to-night."

"We'll need you, Crosby. Don't miss the train."

"I'll be at the station an hour before the train leaves. Confound it, it's a mean trip down there--three hours through the rankest kind of scenery and three hours back. She's visiting in the country, too, but I can drive out and back in an hour."

"On your life, old man, don't fail me."

"Don't worry, Graves; all Christendom couldn't keep me in Dexter after four o'clock this afternoon. Good-by." And Crosby climbed into the hansom and was driven away at breakneck speed toward the station.

Crosby was the junior member of the law firm of Rolfe & Crosby, and his trip to the country was on business connected with the settlement of a big estate. Mrs. Delancy, widow of a son of the decedent, was one of the legatees, and she was visiting her sister-in-law, Mrs. Robert Austin, in central Illinois. Mr. Austin owned extensive farming interests near Dexter, and his handsome home was less than two miles from the heart of the town. Crosby anticipated no trouble in driving to the house and back in time to catch the afternoon train for Chicago. It was necessary for Mrs. Delancy to sign certain papers, and he was confident the transaction could not occupy more than half an hour's time.

At 11:30 Crosby stepped from the coach to the station platform in Dexter, looked inquiringly about, and then asked a perspiring man with a star on his suspender-strap where he could hire a horse and buggy. The officer directed him to a "feed-yard and stable," but observed that there was a "funeral in town an' he'd be lucky if he got a rig, as all of Smith's horses were out." Application at the stable brought the first frown to Crosby's brow. He could not rent a "rig" until after the funeral, and that would make it too late for him to catch the four o'clock train for Chicago. To make the story short, twelve o'clock saw him trudging along the dusty road covering the two miles between town and Austin's place, and he was walking with the rapidity of one who has no love for the beautiful.

The early spring air was invigorating, and it did not take him long to reduce the distance. Austin's house stood on a hill, far back from the highway, and overlooking the entire country-side.

The big red barn stood in from the road a hundred yards or more, and he saw that the same driveway led to the house on the hill. There was no time for speculation, so he hastily made his way up the lane. Crosby had never seen his client, their business having been conducted by mail or through Mr. Rolfe. There was not a person in sight, and he slowed his progress considerably as he drew nearer the big house. At the barn-yard gate he came to a full stop and debated within himself the wisdom of inquiring at the stables for Mr. Austin.

He flung open the gate and strode quickly to the door. This he opened boldly and stepped inside, finding himself in a lofty carriage room. Several handsome vehicles stood at the far end, but the wide space near the door was clear. The floor was as "clean as a pin," except along the west side. No one was in sight, and the only sound was that produced by the horses as they munched their hay and stamped their hoofs in impatient remonstrance with the flies.

"Where the deuce are the people?" he muttered as he crossed to the mangers. "Devilish queer," glancing about in considerable doubt. "The hands must be at dinner or taking a nap." He passed by a row of mangers and was calmly inspected by brown-eyed horses. At the end of the long row of stalls he found a little gate opening into another section of the barn. He was on the point of opening this gate to pass in among the horses when a low growl attracted his attention. In some alarm he took a precautionary look ahead. On the opposite side of the gate stood a huge and vicious looking bulldog, unchained and waiting for him with an eager ferocity that could not be mistaken. Mr. Crosby did not open the gate. Instead he inspected it to see that it was securely fastened, and then drew his hand across his brow.

"What an escape!" he gasped, after a long breath. "Lucky for me you growled, old boy. My name is Crosby, my dear sir, and I'm not here to steal anything. I'm only a lawyer. Anybody else at home but you?"

An ominous growl was the answer, and there was lurid disappointment in the face of the squat figure beyond the gate.

"Come, now, old chap, don't be nasty. I won't hurt you. There was nothing farther from my mind than a desire to disturb you. And say, please do something besides growl. Bark, and oblige me. You may attract the attention of some one."

By this time the ugly brute was trying to get at the man, growling, and snarling savagely. Crosby complacently looked on from his place of safety for a moment, and was on the point of turning away when his attention was caught by a new move on the part of the dog. The animal ceased his violent efforts to get through the gate, turned about deliberately, and raced from view behind the horse stalls. Crosby brought himself up with a jerk.

"Thunder," he ejaculated; "the brute knows a way to get at me, and he won't be long about it, either. What the dickens shall I--by George, this looks serious! He'll head me off at the door if I try to get out and--Ah, the fire-escape! We'll fool you, you brute! What a cursed idiot I was not to go to the house instead of coming--" He was shinning up a ladder with little regard for grace as he mumbled this self-condemnatory remark. There was little dignity in his manner of flight, and there was certainly no glory in the position in which he found himself a moment later. But there was a vast amount of satisfaction.

The ladder rested against a beam that crossed the carriage shed near the middle. The beam was a large one, hewn from a monster tree, and was free on all sides. The ladder had evidently been left there by men who had used it recently and had neglected to return it to the hooks on which it properly hung.

When the dog rushed violently through the door and into the carriage room, he found a vast and inexplicable solitude. He was, to all appearances, alone with the vehicles under which he was permitted to trot when his master felt inclined to grant the privilege.

Crosby, seated on the beam, fifteen feet above the floor, grinned securely but somewhat dubiously as he watched the mystified dog below. At last he laughed aloud. He could not help it. The enemy glanced upward and blinked his red eyes in surprise; then he stared in deep chagrin, then glared with rage. For a few minutes Crosby watched his frantic efforts to leap through fifteen feet of altitudinal space, confidently hoping that some one would come to drive the brute away and liberate him. Finally he began to lose the good humor his strategy in fooling the dog had inspired, and a hurt, indignant stare was directed toward the open door through which he had entered.

"What's the matter with the idiots?" he growled impatiently. "Are they going to let this poor dog snarl his lungs out? He's a faithful chap, too, and a willing worker. Gad, I never saw anything more earnest than the way he tries to climb up that ladder." Adjusting himself in a comfortable position, his elbows on his knees, his hands to his chin, he allowed his feet to swing lazily, tantalizingly, below the beam. "I'm putting a good deal of faith in this beam," he went on resignedly. The timber was at least fifteen inches square.

"Ah, by George! That was a bully jump--the best you've made. You didn't miss me more than ten feet that time. I don't like to be disrespectful, you know, but you are an exceedingly rough looking dog. Don't get huffy about it, old fellow, but you have the ugliest mouth I ever saw. Yes, you miserable cur, politeness at last ceases to be a virtue with me. If I had you up here I'd punch your face for you, too. Why don't you come up, you coward? You're bow-legged, too, and you haven't any more figure than a crab. Anybody that would take an insult like that is beneath me (thank heaven!) and would steal sheep. Great Scott! Where are all these people? Shut up, you brute, you! I'm getting a headache. But it doesn't do any good to reason with you, I can see that plainly. The thing I ought to do is to go down there and punish you severely. But I'll-- Hello! Hey, boy! Call off this--confounded dog."

Two small Lord Fauntleroy boys were standing in the door, gazing up at him with wide open mouths and bulging eyes.

"Call him off, I say, or I'll come down there and kick a hole clear through him." The boys stared all the harder. "Is your name Austin?" he demanded, addressing neither in particular.

"Yes, sir," answered the larger boy, with an effort.

"Well, where's your father? Shut up, you brute! Can't you see I'm talking? Go tell your father I want to see him, boy."

"Dad's up at the house."

"That sounds encouraging. Can't you call off this dog?"

"I--I guess I'd better not. That's what dad keeps him for."

"Oh, he does, eh? And what is it that he keeps him for?"

"To watch tramps."

"To watch--to watch tramps? Say, boy, I'm a lawyer and I'm here on business." He was black in the face with indignation.

"You better come up to the house and see dad, then. He don't live in the barn," said the boy keenly.

"I can't fly to the house, boy. Say, if you don't call off this dog I'll put a bullet through him."

"You'd have to be a purty good shot, mister. Nearly everybody in the county has tried to do it." Both boys were grinning diabolically and the dog took on energy through inspiration. Crosby longed for a stick of dynamite.

"I'll give you a dollar if you get him away from here."

"Let's see your dollar." Crosby drew a silver dollar from his trousers pocket, almost falling from his perch in the effort.

"Here's the coin. Call him off," gasped the lawyer.

"I'm afraid papa wouldn't like it," said the boy. The smaller lad nudged his brother and urged him to "take the money anyhow."

"I live in Chicago," Crosby began, hoping to impress the boys at least.

"So do we when we're at home," said the smaller boy. "We live in Chicago in the winter time."

"Is Mrs. Delancy your aunt?"

"Yes, sir."

"I'll give you this dollar if you'll tell your father I'm here and want to see him at once."

"Throw down your dollar." The coin fell at their feet but rolled deliberately through a crack in the floor and was lost forever. Crosby muttered something unintelligible, but resignedly threw a second coin after the first.

"He'll be out when he gets through dinner," said the older boy, just before the fight. Two minutes later he was streaking across the barn lot with the coin in his pocket, the smaller boy wailing under the woe of a bloody nose. For half an hour Crosby heaped insult after insult upon the glowering dog at the bottom of the ladder and was in the midst of a rabid denunciation of Austin when the city-bred farmer entered the barn.

"Am I addressing Mr. Robert Austin?" called Crosby, suddenly amiable. The dog subsided and ran to his master's side. Austin, a black- moustached, sallow-faced man of forty, stopped near the door and looked aloft, squinting.

"Where are you?" he asked somewhat sharply.

"I am very much up in the air," replied Crosby. "Look a little sou' by sou'east. Ah, now you have me. Can you manage the dog? If so, I'll come down."

"One moment, please. Who are you?"

"My name is Crosby, of Rolfe & Crosby, Chicago. I am here to see Mrs. Delancy, your sister-in-law, on business before she leaves for New York."

"What is your business with her, may I ask?"

"Private," said Crosby laconically. "Hold the dog."

"I insist in knowing the nature of your business," said Austin firmly.

"I'd rather come down there and talk, if you don't mind."

"I don't but the dog may," said the other grimly.

"Well, this is a nice way to treat a gentleman," cried Crosby wrathfully.

"A gentleman would scarcely have expected to find a lady in the barn, much less on a cross-beam. This is where my horses and dogs live."

"Oh, that's all right now; this isn't a joke, you know."

"I quite agree with you. What is your business with Mrs. Delancy?"

"We represent her late husband's interests in settling up the estate of his father. Your wife's interests are being looked after by Morton & Rogers, I believe. I am here to have Mrs. Delancy go through the form of signing papers authorizing us to bring suit against the estate in order to establish certain rights of which you are fully aware. Your wife's brother left his affairs slightly tangled, you remember."

"Well, I can save you a good deal of trouble. Mrs. Delancy has decided to let the matter rest as it is and to accept the compromise terms offered by the other heirs. She will not care to see you, for she has just written to your firm announcing her decision."

"You--you don't mean it," exclaimed Crosby in dismay. He saw a prodigious fee slipping through his fingers. "Gad, I must see her about this," he went on, starting down the ladder, only to go back again hastily. The growling dog leaped forward and stood ready to receive him. Austin chuckled audibly.

"She really can't see you, Mr. Crosby. Mrs. Delancy leaves at four o'clock for

Chicago, where she takes the Michigan Central for New York to-night. You can gain nothing by seeing her."

"But I insist, sir," exploded Crosby.

"You may come down when you like," said Austin. "The dog will be here until I return from the depot after driving her over. Come down when you like."

Crosby did not utter the threat that surged to his lips. With the wisdom born of self-preservation, he temporized, reserving deep down in the surging young breast a promise to amply recompense his pride for the blows it was receiving at the hands of the detestable Mr. Austin.

"You'll admit that I'm in a devil of a pickle, Mr. Austin," he said jovially. "The dog is not at all friendly."

"He is at least diverting. You won't be lonesome while I'm away. I'll tell Mrs. Delancy that you called," said Austin ironically.

He turned to leave the barn, and the sinister sneer on his face gave Crosby a new and amazing inspiration. Like a flash there rushed into his mind the belief that Austin had a deep laid design in not permitting him to see the lady. With this belief also came the conviction that he was hurrying her off to New York on some pretext simply to forestall any action that might induce her to continue the contemplated suit against the estate. Mrs. Delancy had undoubtedly been urged to drop the matter under pressure of promises, and the Austins were getting her away from the scene of action before she could reconsider or before her solicitors could convince her of the mistake she was making. The thought of this sent the fire of resentment racing through Crosby's brain, and he fairly gasped with the longing to get at the bottom of the case. His only hope now lay in sending a telegram to Mr. Rolfe, commanding him to meet Mrs. Delancy when her train reached Chicago, and to lay the whole matter before her.

Before Austin could make his exit the voices of women were heard outside the door and an instant later two ladies entered. The farmer attempted to turn them back, but the younger, taller, and slighter of the newcomers cried:

"I just couldn't go without another look at the horses, Bob."

Crosby, on the beam, did not fail to observe the rich, tender tone of the voice, and it would have required almost total darkness to obscure the beauty of her face. Her companion was older and coarser, and he found delight in the belief that she was the better half of the disagreeable Mr. Austin.

"Good-afternoon, Mrs. Delancy!" came a fine masculine voice from nowhere. The ladies started in amazement, Mr. Austin ground his teeth, the dog took another tired leap upward; Mr. Crosby took off his hat gallantly, and waited patiently for the lady to discover his whereabouts.

"Who is it, Bob?" cried the tall one, and Crosby patted his bump of shrewdness happily. "Who have you in hiding here?"

"I'm not in hiding, Mrs. Delancy. I'm a prisoner, that's all. I'm right near the top of the ladder directly in front of you. You know me only through the mails, but my partner, Mr. Rolfe, is known to you personally. My name is Crosby."

"How very strange," she cried in wonder. "Why don't you come down, Mr. Crosby?"

"I hate to admit it, but I'm afraid. There's the dog, you know. Have you any influence over him?"

"None whatever. He hates me. Perhaps Mr. Austin can manage him. Oh, isn't it ludicrous?" and she burst into hearty laughter. It was a very musical laugh, but Crosby considered it a disagreeable croak.

"But Mr. Austin declines to interfere. I came to see you on private business and am not permitted to do so."

"We don't know this fellow, Louise, and I can't allow you to talk to him," said Austin brusquely. "I found him where he is and there he stays until the marshal comes out from town. His actions have been very suspicious and must be investigated. I can't take chances on letting a horse thief escape. Swallow will watch him until I can secure assistance."

"I implore you, Mrs. Delancy, to give me a moment or two in which to explain," cried Crosby. "He knows I'm not here to steal his horses, and he knows I intend to punch his head the minute I get the chance." Mrs. Austin's little shriek of dismay and her husband's fierce glare did not check the flow of language from the beam. "I AM Crosby of Rolfe & Crosby, your counsel. I have the papers here for you to sign and--"

"Louise, I insist that you come away from here. This fellow is a fraud-- "

"He's refreshing, at any rate," said Mrs. Delancy gaily. "There can be no harm in hearing what he has to say, Bob."

"You are very kind, and I won't detain you long."

"I've a mind to kick you out of this barn," cried Austin angrily.

"I don't believe you're tall enough, my good fellow." Mr. Crosby was more than amiable. He was positively genial. Mrs. Delancy's pretty face was the picture of eager, excited mirth, and he saw that she was determined to see the comedy to the end.

"Louise!" exclaimed Mrs. Austin, speaking for the first time. "You are not fool enough to credit this fellow's story, I'm sure. Come to the house at once. I will not stay here." Mrs. Austin's voice was hard and biting, and Crosby also caught the quick glance that passed between husband and wife.

"I am sure Mrs. Delancy will not be so unkind as to leave me after I've had so much trouble in getting an audience. Here is my card, Mrs. Delancy." Crosby tossed a card from his perch, but Swallow gobbled it up instantly. Mrs. Delancy gave a little cry of disappointment, and Crosby promptly apologized for the dog's greediness. "Mr. Austin knows I'm Crosby," he concluded.

"I know nothing of the sort, sir, and I forbid Mrs. Delancy holding further conversation with you. This is an outrageous imposition, Louise. You must hurry, by the way, or we'll miss the train," said Austin, biting his lip impatiently.

"That reminds me, I also take the four o'clock train for Chicago, Mrs. Delancy. If you prefer, we can talk over our affairs on the train instead of here. I'll confess this isn't a very dignified manner in which to hold a consultation," said Crosby apologetically.

"Will you be kind enough to state the nature of your business, Mr. Crosby?" said the young woman, ignoring Mr. Austin.

"Then you believe I'm Crosby?" cried that gentleman triumphantly.

"Louise!" cried Mrs. Austin in despair.

"In spite of your present occupation, I believe you are Crosby," said Mrs. Delancy merrily.

"But, good gracious, I can't talk business with you from this confounded beam," he cried lugubriously.

"Mr. Austin will call the dog away," she said confidently, turning to the man in the door. Austin's sallow face lighted with a sudden malicious grin, and there was positive joy in his voice.

"You may be satisfied, but I am not. If you desire to transact business with this impertinent stranger, Mrs. Delancy, you'll have to do so under existing conditions. I do not approve of him or his methods, and my dog doesn't either. You can trust a dog for knowing a man for what he is. Mrs. Austin and I are going to the house. You may remain, of course; I have no right to command you to follow. When you are ready to drive to the station, please come to the house. I'll be ready. Your Mr. Crosby may leave when he likes--IF HE CAN. Come, Elizabeth." With this defiant thrust, Mr. Austin stalked from the barn, followed by his wife. Mrs. Delancy started to follow but checked herself immediately, a flush of anger mounting to her brow. After a long pause she spoke.

"I don't understand how you came to be where you are, Mr. Crosby," she said slowly. He related his experiences rapidly and laughed with her simply because she had a way with her.

"You'll pardon me for laughing," she giggled.

"With all my heart," he replied gallantly. "It must be very funny. However, this is not business. You are in a hurry to get away from here and--I'm not, it seems. Briefly, Mrs. Delancy, I have the papers you are to sign before we begin your action against the Fairwater estate. You know what they are through Mr. Rolfe."

"Well, I'm sorry, Mr. Crosby, to say to you that I have decided to abandon the matter. A satisfactory compromise is under way."

"So I've been told. But are you sure you understand yourself?"

"Perfectly, thank you."

"This is a very unsatisfactory place from which to argue my case, Mrs. Delancy. Can't you dispose of the dog?"

"Only God disposes."

"Well, do you mind telling me what the compromise provides?" She stared at him for a moment haughtily, but his smile won the point for him. She told him everything and then looked very much displeased when he swore distinctly.

"Pardon me, but you are getting very much the worst of it in this deal. It is the most contemptible scheme to rob that I ever heard of. By this arrangement you are to get farming lands and building lots in rural towns worth in all about $100,000, I'd say. Don't you know that you are entitled to nearly half a million?"

"Oh, dear, no. By right, my share is less than $75,000," she cried triumphantly.

"Who told you so?" he demanded, and she saw a very heavy frown on his erstwhile merry face.

"Why--why, Mr. Austin and another brother-in-law, Mr. Gray, both of whom are very kind to me in the matter, I'm sure."

"Mrs. Delancy, you are being robbed by these fellows. Can't you see that these brothers-in-law and their wives will profit immensely if they succeed in keeping the wool over your eyes long enough? Let ME show you some figures." He excitedly drew a packet of papers from his pocket and in five minutes' time had her gasping with the knowledge that she was legally entitled to more than half a million of dollars.

"Are you sure?" she cried, unable to believe her ears.

"Absolutely. Here is the inventory and here are the figures to corroborate everything I say."

"But THEY had figures, too," she cried in perplexity.

"Certainly. Figures are wonderful things. I only ask you to defer this plan to compromise until we are able to thoroughly convince you that I am not misrepresenting the facts to you."

"Oh, if I could only believe you!"

"I'd toss the documents down to you if I were not afraid they'd join my card. That is a terribly ravenous beast. Surely you can coax him out of the barn," he added eagerly.

"I can try, but persuasion is difficult with a bulldog, you know," she said doubtfully. "It is much easier to persuade a man," she smiled.

"I trust you won't try to persuade me to come down," he said in alarm.

"Mr. Austin is a brute to treat you in this manner," she cried indignantly.

"I wouldn't treat a dog as he is treating me."

"Oh, I am sure you couldn't," she cried in perfect sincerity. "Swallow doesn't like me, but I'll try to get him away. You can't stay up there all night."

"By Jove!" he exclaimed sharply.

"What is it?" she asked quickly.

"I had forgotten an engagement in Chicago for to-night. Box party at the comic opera," he said, looking nervously at his watch.

"It would be too bad if you missed it," she said sweetly. "You'd be much more comfortable in a box."

"You are consoling at least. Are you going to coax him off?"

"In behalf of the box party, I'll try. Come, Swallow. There's a nice doggie!"

Crosby watched the proceedings with deepest interest and concern and not a little admiration. But not only did Swallow refuse to abdicate but he seemed to take decided exceptions to the feminine method of appeal. He evidently did not like to be called "doggie," "pet," "dearie," and all such.

"He won't come," she cried plaintively.

"I have it!" he exclaimed, his face brightening. "Will you hand me that three-tined pitchfork over there? With that in my hands I'll make Swallow see--Look out! For heaven's sake, don't go near him! He'll kill you." She had taken two or three steps toward the dog, her hand extended pleadingly, only to be met by an ominous growl, a fine display of teeth, and a bristling back. As if paralyzed, she halted at the foot of the ladder, terror suddenly taking possession of her.

"Can you get the pitchfork?"

"I am afraid to move," she moaned. "He is horrible--horrible!"

"I'll come down, Mrs. Delancy, and hang the consequences," Crosby cried, and was suiting the action to the word when she cried out in remonstrance.

"Don't come down--don't! He'll kill you. I forbid you to come down, Mr. Crosby. Look at him! Oh, he's coming toward me! Don't come down!" she shrieked. "I'll come up!"

Grasping her skirts with one hand she started frantically up the ladder, her terrified eyes looking into the face of the man above. There was a vicious snarl from the dog, a savage lunge, and then something closed over her arm like a vice. She felt herself being jerked upward and a second later she was on the beam beside the flushed young man whose strong hand and not the dog's jaws had reached her first. He was obliged to support her for a few minutes with one of his emphatic arms, so near was she to fainting.

"Oh," she gasped at last, looking into his eyes questioningly. "Did he bite me? I was not sure, you know. He gave such an awful leap for me. How did you do it?"

"A simple twist of the wrist, as the prestidigitators say. You had a close call, my dear Mrs. Delancy." He was a-quiver with new sensations that were sending his spirits sky high. After all it was not turning out so badly.

"He would have dragged me down had it not been for you. And I might have been torn to pieces," she shuddered, glancing down at the now infuriated dog.

"It would have been appalling," he agreed, discreetly allowing her to imagine the worst.

"How can I ever thank you?" cried she impulsively. He made a very creditable show of embarrassment in the effort to convince her that he had accomplished only what any man would have attempted under similar circumstances. She was thoroughly convinced that no other man could have succeeded.

"Well, we're in a pretty position, are we not?" he asked in the end.

"I think I can stick on without being held, Mr. Crosby," she said, and his arm slowly and regretfully came to parade rest.

"Are you sure you won't get dizzy?" he demanded in deep solicitude.

"I'll not look down," she said, smiling into his eyes. He lost the power of speech for a moment. "May I look at those figures now?"

For the next ten minutes she studiously followed him as he explained the contents of the various papers. She held the sheets and they sat very close to each other on the big beam. The dog looked on in sour disgust.

"They cannot be wrong," she cried at last. Her eyes were sparkling. "You are as good as an angel."

"I only regret that I can't complete the illusion by unfolding a strong and convenient pair of wings," he said dolorously. "How are we to catch that train for Chicago?"

"I'm afraid we can't," she said demurely. "You'll miss the box party."

"That's a pleasure easily sacrificed."

"Besides, you are seeing me on business. Pleasure should never interfere with business, you know."

"It doesn't seem to," he said, and the dog saw them smile tranquilly into each other's eyes.

"Oh, isn't this too funny for words?" He looked very grateful.

"I wonder when Austin will condescend to release us."

"I have come to a decision, Mr. Crosby," she said irrelevantly.

"Indeed?"

"I shall never speak to Robert Austin again, and I'll never enter his house as long as I live," she announced determinedly.

"Good! But you forget your personal effects. They are in his house." He was overflowing with happiness.

"They have all gone to the depot and I have the baggage checks. My ticket and my money are in this purse. You see, we are quite on the same footing."

"I don't feel sure of my footing," he commented ruefully. "By the way, I have a fountain pen. Would you mind signing these papers? We'll be quite sure of our standing at least."

She deliberately spread out the papers on the beam, and, while he obligingly kept her from falling, signed seven documents in a full, decisive hand: "Louise Hampton Delancy."

"There! That means that you are to begin suit," she said finally, handing the pen to him.

"I'll not waste an instant," he said meaningly. "In fact, the suit is already under way."

"I don't understand you," she said, but she flushed.

"That's what a lawyer says when he goes to court," he explained.

"Oh," she said, thoroughly convinced.

At the end of another hour the two on the beam were looking at each other with troubled eyes. When he glanced at his watch at six o'clock, his face was extremely sober. There was a tired, wistful expression in her eyes.

"Do you think they'll keep us here all night?" she asked plaintively.

"Heaven knows what that scoundrel will do."

"We have the papers signed, at any rate." She sighed, trying to revive the dying spark of humor.

"And we won't be lonesome," he added, glaring at the dog.

"Did you ever dream that a man could be so despicable?"

"Ah, here comes some one at last," he cried, brightening up.

The figure of Robert Austin appeared in the doorway.

"Oho, you're both up there now, are you?" he snapped. "That's why you didn't go to the depot, is it? Well, how has the business progressed?"

"She has signed all the papers, if that's what you want to know," said Crosby tantalizingly.

"That's all the good it will do her. We'll beat you in court, Mr. Crosby, and we won't leave a dollar for you, my dear sister-in-law," snarled Austin, his face white with rage.

"And now that we've settled our business, and missed our train, perhaps you'll call off your confounded dog," said Crosby. Austin's face broke into a wide grin, and he chuckled aloud. Then he leaned against the door-post and held his sides.

"What's the joke?" demanded the irate Crosby. Mrs. Delancy clasped his arm and looked down upon Austin as if he had suddenly gone mad.

"You want to come down, eh?" cackled Austin. "Why don't you come down? I know you'll pardon my laughter, but I have just remembered that you may be a horse thief and that I was not going to let you escape. Mrs. Delancy refuses to speak to me, so I decline to ask her to come down."

"Do you mean to say you'll keep this lady up here for--" began Crosby fiercely. Her hand on his arm prevented him from leaping to the floor.

"She may come down when she desires, and so may you, sir," roared Austin stormily.

"But some one will release us, curse you, and then I'll make you sorry you ever lived," hissed Crosby. "You are a black-hearted cur, a cowardly dog--"

"Don't--don't!" whispered the timid woman beside him.

"You are helping your cause beautifully," sneered Austin. "My men have instructions to stay away from the barn until the marshal comes. I, myself, expect to feed and bed the horses."

Deliberately he went about the task of feeding the horses. The two on the beam looked on in helpless silence. Crosby had murder in his heart. At last the master of the situation started for the door.

"Good-night," he said sarcastically. "Pleasant dreams."

"You brute," cried Crosby, hoarse with anger. A sob came from his tired companion and Crosby turned to her, his heart full of tenderness and-- shame, perhaps. Tears were streaming down her cheeks and her shoulders drooped dejectedly.

"What shall we do?" she moaned. Crosby could frame no answer. He gently took her hand in his and held it tightly. She made no effort to withdraw it.

"I'm awfully sorry," he said softly. "Don't cry, little woman. It will all end right,

I know."

Just then Austin reentered the barn. Without a word he strode over and emptied a pan of raw meat on the floor in front of the dog. Then he calmly departed, but Crosby could have sworn he heard him chuckle. The captives looked at each other dumbly for a full minute, one with wet, wide-open, hurt eyes, the other with consternation. Gradually the sober light in their eyes faded away and feeble smiles developed into peals of laughter. The irony of the situation bore down upon them irresistibly and their genuine, healthy young minds saw the picture in all of its ludicrous colorings. Not even the prospect of a night in mid-air could conquer the wild desire to laugh.

"Isn't it too funny for words?" she laughed bravely through her tears.

Then, for some reason, both relapsed into dark, silent contemplation of the dog who was so calmly enjoying his evening repast.

"I am sorry to admit it, Mr. Crosby, but I am growing frightfully hungry," she said wistfully.

"It has just occurred to me that I haven't eaten a bite since seven o'clock this morning," he said.

"You poor man! I wish I could cook something for you."

"You might learn."

"You know what I mean," she explained, reddening a bit. "You must be nearly famished."

"I prefer to think of something more interesting," he said coolly.

"It is horrid!" she sobbed. "See, it is getting dark. Night is coming. Mr. Crosby, what is to become of us?" He was very much distressed by her tears and a desperate resolve took root in his breast. She was so tired and dispirited that she seemed glad when he drew her close to him and pressed her head upon his shoulder. He heard the long sigh of relief and relaxation and she peered curiously over her wet lace handkerchief when he muttered tenderly:

"Poor little chap!"

Then she sighed again quite securely, and there was a long silence, broken regularly and rhythmically by the faint little catches that once were tearful sobs.

"Oh, dear me! It is quite dark," she cried suddenly, and he felt a shudder run through her body.

"Where could you go to-night, Mrs. Delancy, if we were to succeed in getting away from here?" he asked abruptly. She felt his figure straighten and his arm grow tense as if a sudden determination had charged through it.

"Why--why, I hadn't thought about that," she confessed, confronted by a new proposition.

"There's a late night train for Chicago," he volunteered.

"But how are we to catch it?"

"If you are willing to walk to town I think you can catch it," he said, a strange ring in his voice.

"What do you mean?" she demanded, looking up at his face quickly.

"Can you walk the two miles?" he persisted. "The train leaves Dexter at eleven o'clock and it is now nearly eight."

"Of course I can walk it," she said eagerly. "I could walk a hundred miles to get away from this place."

"You'll miss the New York train, of course."

"I've changed my mind, Mr. Crosby. I shall remain in Chicago until we have had our revenge on Austin and the others."

"That's very good of you. May I ask where you stop in Chicago?"

"My apartments are in the C--- Building. My mother lives with me."

"Will you come to see me some time?" he asked, an odd smile on his lips.

"Come to see you?" she cried in surprise. "The idea! What do you mean?"

"I may not be able to call on you for some time, but you can be very good to me by coming to see me. I'll be stopping at St. Luke's Hospital for quite a while."

"At St. Luke's Hospital? I don't understand," she cried perplexed.

"You see, my dear Mrs. Delancy, I have come to a definite conclusion in regard to our present position. You must not stay here all night. I'd be a coward and a cur to subject you to such a thing. Well, I'm going down to tackle that dog."

"To--tackle--the--dog," she gasped.

"And while I'm keeping him busy you are to cut and run for the road down there. Then you'll have easy sailing for town."

"Mr. Crosby," she said firmly, clasping his arm; "you are not to leave this beam. Do you think I'll permit you to go down there and be torn to pieces by that beast, just for the sake of letting me cut and run, as you call it? I'd be a bigger brute than the dog and--and--"

"Mrs. Delancy, my mind is made up. I'm going down!"

"That settles it! I'm coming too," she proclaimed emphatically.

"To be sure. That's the plan. You'll escape while I hold Swallow."

"I'll do nothing of the sort. You shall not sacrifice yourself for my sake. I'd stay up here with you all the rest of my life before I'd permit you to do that."

"I'll remind you of that offer later on, my dear Mrs. Delancy, when we are not so pressed for time. Just now you must be practical, however. We can't stay up here all night."

"Please, Mr. Crosby, for my sake, don't go down there. To please me, don't be disfigured. I know you are awfully brave and strong, but he is such a huge, vicious dog. Won't you please stay here?"

"Ten minutes from now it will be too dark to see the dog and he'll have an advantage over me. Listen: I'll meet you at the depot in an hour and a half. This is final, Mrs. Delancy. Will you do as I tell you? Run for the road and then to town. I'll promise to join you there."

"Oh, dear! Oh, dear!" she moaned, as he drew away from her and swung one foot to the ladder. "I shall die if you go down there."

"I am going just the same. Don't be afraid, little woman. My pocket knife is open and it is a trusty blade. Now, be brave and be quick. Follow me down the ladder and cut for it."

"Please, please, please!" she implored, wringing her hands.

But he was already half-way down the ladder and refused to stop.

Suddenly Crosby paused as if checked in his progress by some insurmountable obstacle. The dog was at the foot of the ladder, snarling with joy over the prospective end of his long vigil. Above, Mrs. Delancy was moaning and imploring him to come back to her side, even threatening to spring from the beam to the floor before he could reach the bottom.

"By George!" he exclaimed, and then climbed up three or four rounds of the ladder, greatly to the annoyance of the dog.

"What is it?" cried Mrs. Delancy, recovering her balance on the beam.

"Let me think for a minute," he answered, deliberately resting his elbow on an upper round.

"It is about time you were doing a little thinking," she said, relief and asperity in her voice. "In another second I should have jumped into that dog's jaws."

"I believe it can be done," he went on, excited enthusiasm growing in his voice. "That's what bulldogs are famous for, isn't it?"

"I don't know what you are talking about, but I do know that whenever they take hold of anything they have to be treated for lockjaw before they will let go. If you don't come up here beside me I'll have a fit, Mr. Crosby."

"That's it--that's what I mean," he cried eagerly. "If they close those jaws upon anything they won't let go until death them doth part. Gad, I believe I see a way out of this pickle."

"I don't see how that can help us. The dog's jaws are the one and only obstacle, and it is usually the other fellow's death that parts them. Oh," she went on, plaintively, "if we could only pull his teeth. Good heaven, Mr. Crosby," sitting up very abruptly, "you are not thinking of undertaking it, are you?"

"No, but I've got a scheme that will make Swallow ashamed of himself to the end of his days. I can't help laughing over it." He leaned back and laughed heartily. "Hold my coat, please." He removed his coat quickly and passed it up to her.

"I insist on knowing what you intend doing," she exclaimed.

"Just wait and see me show Mr. Swallow a new trick or two." He had already taken his watch and chain, his fountain pen, and other effects from his vest, jamming them into his trousers pockets. Mrs. Delancy, in the growing darkness, looked on, puzzled and anxious.

"You might tell me," she argued resentfully. "Are you going to try to swim out?"

Folding the vest lengthwise, he took a firm grip on the collar, and cautiously descended the ladder.

"I'll not come to the hospital," she cried warningly. "Don't! he'll bite your leg off!"

"I'm merely teasing him, Mrs. Delancy. He sha'n't harm my legs, don't fear. Now watch for developments." Pausing just beyond reach of the dog's mightiest leaps, he took a firm hold on the ladder and swung down with the vest until it almost slapped the head of the angry animal. It was like casting a fly directly at the head of a hungry pickerel. Swallow's eager jaws closed down upon the cloth and the teeth met like a vice. The heavy body of the brute almost jerked Crosby's arm from the socket, but he braced himself, recovered his poise, and clung gaily to the ladder, with the growling, squirming dog dangling free of the floor. Mrs. Delancy gave a little shriek of terror.

"Are you--going to bring him up here?" she gasped.

"Heaven knows where he'll end."

"But he will ruin your vest."

"I'll charge it up to your account. Item: one vest, fifteen dollars."

By this time he was swinging Swallow slowly back and forth, and he afterwards said that it required no little straining of his muscles.

"You extravagant thing!" she cried, but did not tell whether she meant his profligacy in purchasing or his wantonness in destroying. "And now, pray enlighten me. Are you swinging him just for fun or are you crazy?"

"Everything depends on his jaws and my strong right arm," he said, and he was beginning to pant from the exertion. Swallow was swinging higher and higher.

"Well, it is the most aimless proceeding I ever saw."

"I hope not. On second thought, everything depends on my aim."

"And what is your aim, Mr. Hercules?"

"See that opening above the box-stall over there?"

"Dimly."

"That's my aim. Heavens, he's a heavy brute."

"Oh, I see!" she cried ecstatically, clapping her hands. "Delicious! Lovely! Oh, Mr. Crosby, you are so clever."

"Don't fall off that beam, please," he panted. "It might rattle me."

"I can't help being excited. It is the grandest thing I ever heard of. He can't get out of there, can he? Dear me, the sides of that stall are more than eight feet high."

"He can't--get--out--of it if--I get him--in," gasped Crosby.

Not ten feet away to the left and some four feet above the floor level there was a wide opening into a box-stall, the home of Mr. Austin's prize stallion. As the big horse was inside munching his hay, Crosby was reasonably sure that the stall with its tall sides was securely closed and bolted.

Suddenly there was a mighty creak of the ladder, the swish of a heavy body through the air, an interrupted growl, and then a ripping thud. Swallow's chubby body shot squarely through the opening, accompanied by a trusty though some-what sadly stretched vest, and the deed was done. A cry of delight came from the beam, a shout of pride and relief from the ladder, and sounds of a terrific scramble from the stall. First there was a sickening grunt, then a surprised howl, then the banging of horse- hoofs, and at last a combination of growls and howls that proved Swallow's invasion of a hornet's nest.

"Thunderation!" came in sharp, agonized tones from the ladder.

"What is the matter?" she cried, detecting disaster in the exclamation.

"I am a--a--blooming idiot," he groaned. "I forgot to remove a roll of bills from an upper pocket in that vest!"

"Oh, is that all?" she cried, in great relief, starting down the ladder.

"All? There was at least fifty dollars in that roll," he said, from the floor, not forgetting to assist her gallantly to the bottom.

"You can add it to my bill, you know," she said sweetly.

"But it leaves me dead broke."

"You forget that I have money, Mr. Crosby. What is mine to-night is also yours. I think we should shake hands and congratulate one another." Crosby's sunny na-ture lost its cloud in an instant, and the two clasped hands at the bottom of the ladder.

"I think it is time to cut and run," he said. "It's getting so beastly dark we won't be able to find the road."

"And there is no moon until midnight. But come; we are free. Let us fly the hated spot, as they say in the real novels. How good the air feels!"

She was soon leading the way swiftly toward the gate. Night had fallen so quickly that they were in utter darkness. There were lights in the windows of the house on the hill, and the escaped prisoners, with one impulse, shook their clenched hands toward them.

"I am awfully sorry, Mr. Crosby, that you have endured so much hardship in coming to see me," she went on. "I hope you haven't many such clients as I."

"One is enough, I assure you," he responded, and somehow she took it as a compliment.

"I suppose our next step is to get to the railway station," she said.

"Unless you will condescend to lead me through this assortment of plows, woodpiles, and farm-wagons, I'm inclined to think my next step will be my last. Was ever night so dark?" Her warm, strong fingers clutched his arm and then dropped to his hand. In this fashion she led him swiftly through the night, down a short embankment, and into the gravel highway. "The way looks dark and grewsome ahead of us, Mrs. Delancy. As your lawyer, I'd advise you to turn back and find safe lodging with the enemy. It is going to storm, I'm sure."

"That's your advice as a lawyer, Mr. Crosby. Will you give me your advice as a friend?" she said lightly. Although the time had passed when her guiding hand was necessary, he still held the member in his own.

"I couldn't be so selfish," he protested, and without another word they started off down the road toward town.

"Do you suppose they are delaying the opera in Chicago until you come?" she asked.

"Poor Graves! he said he'd kill me if I didn't come," said Crosby, laughing.

"How dreadful!"

"But I'm not regretting the opera. Quive does not sing until to-morrow night."

"I adore Quive."

"You can't possibly have an engagement for to-morrow night either," he said reflectively.

"I don't see how I could. I expected to be on a Pullman sleeper."

"I'll come for you at 8:15 then."

"You are very good, Mr. Crosby, but I have another plan."

"I beg your pardon for presuming to--" he began, and a hot flush mounted to his brow.

"You are to come at seven for dinner," she supplemented delightedly.

"What a nice place the seventh heaven is!" he cried warmly.

"Sh!" she whispered suddenly, and both stopped stock-still. "There is a man with a lantern at the lower gate. See? Over yonder."

"They're after me, Mrs. Delancy," he whispered. A moment later they were off the road and in the dense shadow of the hedge.

"Is he still in the barn, Mr. Austin?" demanded the man in the buggy.

"I am positive he is. No human being could get away from that dog of mine."

Crosby chuckled audibly, and Mrs. Delancy with difficulty suppressed a proud giggle.

"Well, we might as well go up and get him then. Do you think he's a desperate character?"

"I don't know anything about him, Davis. He says he is a lawyer, but his actions were so strange that I thought you'd best look into his case. A night in the jail won't hurt him, and if he can prove that he is what he says he is, let him go to-morrow. On the other hand, he may turn out to be a very important capture."

"Oh, this is rich!" whispered Crosby excitedly. "Austin is certainly doing the job up brown. But wait till he consults Swallow, the infallible; he won't be so positive." For a few minutes the party of men at the gate conversed in low tones, the listeners being able to catch but few of the words uttered.

"Please let go of my arm, Mrs. Delancy," said Crosby suddenly.

"Where are you going?"

"I am going to tell Austin what I think of him. You don't expect me to stand by and allow a pack of jays to hunt me down as if I were Jesse James or some other desperado, do you?"

"Do you suppose they would credit your story? They will throw you into jail and there you'd stay until some one came down from Chicago to identify you."

"But a word from you would clear me," he said in surprise.

"If they pinned me down to the truth, I could only say I had never seen you until this afternoon."

"Great Scott! You know I am Crosby, don't you?"

"I am positive you are, but what would you, as a lawyer, say to me if you were cross-examining me on the witness stand? You'd ask some very embarrassing questions, and I could only say in the end that the suspected horse thief told me his name and I was goose enough to believe him. No, my dear friend, I think the safest plan is to take advantage of the few minutes' start we have and escape the law."

"You mean that I must run from these fellows as if I were really a thief?"

"Only a suspected thief, you know."

"I'd rather be arrested a dozen times than to desert you at this time."

"Oh, but I'm going with you," she said positively.

"Like a thief, too? I could not permit that, you know. Just stop and think how awkward for you it would be if we were caught flying together."

"Birds of a feather. It might have been worse if you had not disposed of Swallow."

"I must tell you what a genuine brick you are. If they overtake us it will give me the greatest delight in the world to fight the whole posse for your sake."

"After that, do you wonder I want to go with you?" she whispered, and Crosby would have fought a hundred men for her.

The marshal and his men were now following Mr. Austin and the lantern toward the barn, and the road was quite deserted. Mrs. Delancy and Crosby started off rapidly in the direction of the town. The low rumble of distant thunder came to their ears, and ever and anon the western blackness was faintly illumined by flashes of lightning. Neither of the fugitives uttered a word until they were far past the gate.

"By George, Mrs. Delancy, we are forgetting one important thing," said Crosby. They were striding along swiftly arm in arm. "They'll discover our flight, and the railway station will be just where they'll expect to find us."

"Oh, confusion! We can't go to the station, can we?"

"We can, but we'll be captured with humiliating ease."

"I know what we can do. Scott Higgins is the tenant on my farm, and he lives half a mile farther from town than Austin. We can turn back to his place, but we will have to cut across one of Mr. Austin's fields."

"Charming. We can have the satisfaction of trampling on some of Mr. Austin's early wheat crop. Right about, face! But, incidentally, what are we to do after we get to Mr. Higgins's?" They were now scurrying back over the ground they had just traversed.

"Oh, dear me, why should we think about troubles until we come to them?"

"I wasn't thinking about troubles. I'm thinking about something to eat."

"You are intensely unromantic. But Mrs. Higgins is awfully good. She will give us eggs and cakes and milk and coffee and--everything. Won't it be jolly?"

Five minutes later they were plunging through a field of partly grown wheat, in what she averred to be the direction of the Higgins home. It was not good walking, but they were young and strong and very much interested in one another and the adventure.

"Hello, what's this? A river?" he cried, as the swish of running waters came to his ears.

"Oh; isn't it dreadful? I forgot this creek was here, and there is no bridge nearer than a mile. What shall we do? See there is a light in Higgins's house over there. Isn't it disgusting? I could sit down and cry," she wailed. In the distance a dog was heard barking fiercely, but they did not recognize the voice of Swallow. A new trouble confronted them.

"Don't do that," he said resignedly. "Remember how Eliza crossed the ice with the bloodhounds in full trail. Do you know how deep and wide the creek is?"

"It's a tiny bit of a thing, but it's wet," she said ruefully.

"I'll carry you over." And a moment later he was splashing through the shallow brook, holding the lithe, warm figure of his client high above the water. As he set her down upon the opposite bank she gave a pretty sigh of satisfaction, and naively told him that he was very strong for a man in the last stages of starvation.

Two or three noisy dogs gave them the first welcome, and Crosby sagely looked aloft for refuge. His companion quieted the dogs, however, and the advance on the squat farmhouse was made without resistance. The visitors were not long in acquainting the good-natured and astonished young farmer with the situation. Mrs. Higgins was called from her bed and in a jiffy was bustling about the kitchen, from which soon floated odors so tantalizing that the refugees could scarcely suppress the desire to rush forth and storm the good cook in her castle.

"It's mighty lucky you got here when you did, Mrs. Delancy," said Higgins, peering from the window. "Looks 's if it might rain before long. We ain't got much of a place here, but, if you'll put up with it, I guess we can take keer of you over night."

"Oh, but we couldn't think of it," she protested. "After we have had something to eat we must hurry off to the station."

"What station?" asked Crosby sententiously.

"I don't know, but it wouldn't be a bit nice to spoil the adventure by stopping now."

"But we can't walk all over the State of Illinois," he cried.

"For shame! You are ready to give up the instant something to eat comes in sight. Mr. Higgins may be able to suggest something. What is the nearest----"

"I have it," interrupted Crosby. "The Wabash road runs through this neighborhood, doesn't it? Well, where is its nearest station?"

"Lonesomeville--about four miles south," said Higgins.

"Do the night trains stop there?"

"I guess you can flag 'em."

"There's an east-bound train from St. Louis about midnight, I'm quite sure."

While the fugitives were enjoying Mrs. Higgins's hastily but adorably prepared meal, the details of the second stage of the flight were perfected. Mr. Higgins gladly consented to hitch up his high-boarded farm wagon and drive them to the station on the Wabash line, and half an hour later Higgins's wagon clattered away in the night. To all appearances he was the only passenger. But seated on a soft pile of grain sacks in the rear of the wagon, completely hidden from view by the tall "side-beds," were the refugees. Mrs. Delancy insisted upon this mode of travel as a precaution against the prying eyes of persistent marshal's men. Hidden in the wagon-bed they might reasonably escape detection, she argued, and Crosby humored her for more reasons than one. Higgins threw a huge grain tarpaulin over the wagon-bed, and they were sure to be dry in case the rainstorm came as expected. It was so dark that neither could see the face of the other. He had a longing desire to take her hand into his, but there was something in the atmosphere that warned him against such a delightful but unnecessary proceeding. Naturally, they were sitting quite close to each other; even the severe jolting of the springless wagon could not disturb the feeling of happy contentment.

"I hope it won't storm," she said nervously, as a little shudder ran through her body. The wind was now blowing quite fiercely and those long-distant rolls of thunder were taking on the sinister sound of near- by crashes. "I don't mind thunder when I'm in the house."

"And under the bed, I suppose," he laughed.

"Well, you know, lightning COULD strike this wagon," she persisted. "Oh, goodness, that was awfully close!" she cried, as a particularly loud crash came to their ears.

The wagon came to an abrupt stop, and Crosby was about to crawl forth to demand the reason when the sound of a man's voice came through the rushing wind.

"What is it?" whispered Mrs. Delancy, clutching his arm.

"Sh!" he replied. "We're held up by highwaymen, I think!"

"Oh, how lovely!" she whispered rapturously.

"How far are you goin'?" came the strange voice from the night.

"Oh, 's far ag'in as half," responded Higgins warily.

"That you, Scott?" demanded the other.

"Yep."

"Say, Scott, gimme a ride, will you? Goin' as far as Lonesomeville?"

"What you doin' out this time o' night?" demanded Higgins.

"Lookin' for a feller that tried to steal Mr. Austin's horses. We thought we had him cornered up to the place, but he got away somehow. But we'll get him. Davis has got fifty men scouring the country, I bet. I been sent on to Lonesomeville to head him off if he tries to take a train. He's a purty desperate character, they say, too, Scott. Say, gimme a lift as far as you're agoin', won't you?"

"I--I--well, I reckon so," floundered the helpless Higgins.

"Really, this is getting a bit serious," whispered Crosby to his breathless companion.

The deputy was now on the seat with Higgins, and the latter, bewildered and dismayed beyond expression, was urging his horses into their fastest trot.

"How far is it to Lonesomeville?" asked the deputy.

"'Bout two mile."

"It'll rain before we get there," said the other significantly.

"I'm not afeared of rain," said Higgins.

"What are you goin' over there this time o' night for?" asked the other. "You ain't got much of a load."

"I'm--I'm takin' some meat over to Mr. Talbert."

"Hams?"

"No; jest bacon," answered Scott, and his two hearers in the wagon-bed laughed silently.

"Not many people out a night like this," volunteered the deputy.

"Nope."

"That a tarpaulin you got in the back of the bed? Jest saw it by the lightnin'."

"Got the bacon kivered to keep it from gittin' wet 'n case it rains," hastily interposed Scott. He was discussing within himself the advisability of knocking the deputy from the seat and whipping the team into a gallop, leaving him behind.

"You don't mind my crawlin' under the tarpaulin if it rains, do you, Scott?"

"There ain't no--no room under it, Harry, an' I won't allow that bacon to git wet under no consideration."

A generous though nerve-racking crash of thunder changed the current of conversation. It drifted from the weather immediately, however, to a one-sided discussion of the escaped horse thief.

"I guess he's a purty slick one," they heard the deputy say. "Austin said he had him dead to rights in his barn! That big bulldog of his had him treed on a beam, but when we got there, just after dark, the darned cuss was gone, an' the dog was trapped up in a box-stall. By thunder, it showed how desperate the feller is. He evidently come down from that beam an' jest naturally picked that turrible bulldog up by the neck an' throwed him over into the stall."

"Have you got a revolver?" asked Higgins loudly.

"Sure! You don't s'pose I'd go up against that kind of a man without a gun, do you?"

"Oh, goodness!" some one whispered in Crosby's ear.

"But he ain't armed," argued Higgins. "If he'd had a gun don't you s'pose he'd shot that dog an' got away long before he did?"

"That shows how much you know about these crooks, Higgins," said the other loftily. "He had a mighty good reason for not shooting the dog."

"What was the reason?"

"I don't know jest what it was, but any darned fool ought to see that he had a reason. Else why didn't he shoot? Course he had a reason. But the funny part of the whole thing is what has become of the woman."

"What woman?"

"That widder," responded the other, and Crosby felt her arm harden. "I never thought much o' that woman. You'd think she owned the whole town of Dexter to see her paradin' around the streets, showin' off her city clothes, an' all such stuff. They do say she led George Delancy a devil of a life, an' it's no wonder he died."

"The wretch!" came from the rear of the wagon.

"Well, she's up and skipped out with the horse thief. Austin says she tried to protect him, and I guess they had a regular family row over the affair. She's gone an' the man's gone, an' it looks darned suspicious. He was a good-lookin' feller, Austin says, an' she's dead crazy to git another man, I've heard. Dang me, it's jest as I said to Davis: I wouldn't put it above her to take up with this good-lookin' thief an' skip off with him. Her husband's been dead more'n two year, an' she's too darned purty to stay in strict mournin' longer'n she has to---"

But just then something strong, firm, and resistless grasped his neck from behind, and, even as he opened his mouth to gasp out his surprise and alarm, a vise-like grip shut down on his thigh, and then, he was jerked backward, lifted upward, tossed outward, falling downward. The wagon clattered off in the night, and a tall man and a woman looked over the side of the wagon-bed and waited for the next flash of lightning to show them where the official gossiper had fallen. The long, blinding, flash came, and Crosby saw the man as he picked himself from the ditch at the roadside.

"Whip up, Higgins, and we'll leave him so far behind he'll never catch us," cried Crosby eagerly. The first drops of rain began to fall and Mrs. Delancy hurriedly crawled beneath the tarpaulin, urging him to follow at once. Another flash of lightning revealed the deputy, far back in the road waving his hands frantically.

"I'm glad his neck isn't broken. Hurry on, Mr. Higgins; it is now more urgent than ever that you save your bacon."

"'Tain't very comfortable ridin' for Mrs. Delancy," apologized Higgins, his horses in a lope.

"If the marshal asks you why you didn't stop and help his deputy, just tell him that the desperado held a pistol at your head and commanded you to drive like the devil. Holy mackerel, here comes the deluge!"

An instant later he was under the tarpaulin, crouching beside his fellow fugitive. Conversation was impossible, so great was the noise of the rain-storm and the rattle of the wagon over the hard pike. He did his best to protect her from the jars and bumps incident to the leaping and jolting of the wagon, and both were filled with rejoicing when Higgins shouted "Whoa!" to the horses and brought the wild ride to an end.

"Where are we?" cried Crosby, sticking his head from beneath the tarpaulin.

"We're in the dump-shed of the grain elevator, just across the track from the depot."

"And the ride is over?"

"Yep. Did you get bumped much?"

"It was worse, a thousand times, than sitting on the beam," bemoaned a sweet, tired voice, and a moment later the two refugees stood erect in the wagon, neither quite sure that legs so tired and stiff could serve as support.

"It was awful; wasn't it?" Crosby said, stretching himself painfully.

"Are you not drenched to the skin, Mr. Higgins?" cried Mrs. Delancy anxiously. "How selfish of us not to have thought of you before!"

"Oh, that's all right. This gum coat kept me purty dry."

He and Crosby assisted her from the wagon, and, while the former gave his attention to the wet and shivering horses, the latter took her arm and walked up and down the dark shed with her.

"I think you are regretting the impulse that urged you into this folly," he was saying.

"If you persist in accusing me of faintheartedness, Mr. Crosby, I'll never speak to you again," she said. "I cast my lot with a desperado, as the deputy insinuated, and I am sure you have not heard me bewail my fate. Isn't it worth something to have one day and night of real adventure? My gown must be a sight, and I know my hair is just dreadful, but my heart is gayer and brighter to-night than it has been in years."

"And you don't regret anything that has happened?" he asked, pressing her arm ever so slightly.

"My only regret is that you heard what the deputy said about me. You don't believe I am like that, do you?" There was sweet womanly concern in her voice.

"I wish it were light enough to see your face," he answered, his lips close to her ear. "I know you are blushing, and you must be more beautiful--Oh, no, of course I don't think you are at all as he painted you," he concluded, suddenly checking himself and answering the plaintive question he had almost ignored.

"Thank you, kind sir," she said lightly, but he failed not to observe the tinge of confusion in the laugh that followed.

"If you'll watch the team, Mr. Crosby," the voice of Higgins broke in at this timely juncture, "I'll run acrost to the depot an' ast about the train."

"Much obliged, old man; much obliged," returned Crosby affably. "Are you afraid to be alone in the dark?" he asked, as Higgins rushed out into the rain. The storm had abated by this time and there was but the faintest suggestion of distant thunder and lightning, the after-fall of rain being little more than a drizzle.

"Awfully," she confessed, "but it's safer here than on the beam," she added, and his heart grew very tender as he detected the fatigue in her voice. "Anyhow, we have the papers safely signed."

"Mrs. Delancy, I--I swear that you shall never regret this day and night," he said, stopping in his walk and placing his hands on her shoulders. She caught her breath quickly. "Do you know what I mean?"

"I--I think--I'm not quite sure," she stammered.

"You will know some day," he said huskily.

When Mr. Higgins appeared at the end of the shed, carrying a lighted lantern, he saw a tall young man and a tall young woman standing side by side, awaiting his approach with the unconcern of persons who have no interest in common.

"Ah, a lantern," cried Crosby. "Now we can see what we look like and-- and who we are."

Higgins informed them that an east-bound passenger train went through in twenty minutes, stopping on the side track to allow west-bound No. 7 to pass. This train also took water near the bridge which crossed the river just west of the depot. The west-bound train was on time, the other about five minutes late. He brought the welcome news that the rain was over and that a few stars were peeping through the western sky. There was unwelcome news, however, in the statement that the mud was ankle deep from the elevator to the station platform and that the washing out of a street culvert would prevent him from using the wagon.

"I don't mind the mud," said Mrs. Delancy, very bravely indeed.

"My dear Mrs. Delancy, I can and will carry you a mile or more rather than have one atom of Lonesomeville mud bespatter those charming boots of yours," said Crosby cheerfully, and her protestations were useless against the argument of both men.

The distance was not great from the sheds to the station and was soon covered. Crosby was muddy to his knees, but his fair passenger was as dry as toast when he lowered her to the platform.

"You are every bit as strong as the hero in the modern novel," she said gaily. "After this, I'll believe every word the author says about his stalwart, indomitable hero."

To say that Higgins was glad to be homeward bound would be putting it too mildly. The sigh of relief that came from him as he drove out of town a few minutes later was so audible that he heard it himself and smiled contentedly. If he expected to meet the unlamented Harry Brown on the home trip, he was to be agreeably disappointed. Mr. Brown was not on the roadway. He was, instead, on the depot platform at Lonesomeville, and when the westbound express train whistled for the station he was standing grimly in front of two dumbfounded young people who sat sleepily and unwarily on a baggage truck.

The feeble-eyed lantern sat on the platform near Crosby's swinging feet, and the picture that it looked upon was one suggestive of the cheap, sensational, and bloodcurdling border drama. A mud-covered man stood before the trapped fugitives, a huge revolver in his hand, the muzzle of which, even though it wobbled painfully, was uncomfortably close to Mr. Crosby's nose.

"Throw up your hands!" said Brown, his hoarse voice shaking perceptibly. Crosby's hands went up instantly, for he was a man and a diplomat.

"Point it the other way!" cried the lady, with true feminine tact. "How dare you!--Oh, will it go off? Please, please put it away! We won't try to escape!"

"I'm takin' no chances on this feller," said Brown grimly. "It won't go off, ma'am, unless he makes a move to git away."

"What do you want?" demanded Crosby indignantly. "My money? Take it, if you like, but don't be long about it."

"I'm no robber, darn you."

"Well, what in thunder do you mean then by holding me up at the point of a revolver?"

"I'm an officer of the law an' I arrest you. That's what I'm here for," said Brown.

"Arrest me?" exclaimed Crosby in great amazement. "What have I done?"

"No back talk now, young feller. You're the man we're after, an' it won't do you any good to chew the rag about it."

"If you don't turn that horrid pistol away, I'll faint," cried femininity in collapse. Crosby's arm went about her waist and she hid her terror-stricken eyes on his shoulder.

"Keep that hand up!" cried Brown threateningly.

"Don't be mean about it, old man. Can't you see that my arm is not at all dangerous?"

"I've got to search you."

"Search me? Well, I guess not. Where is your authority?"

"I'm a deputy marshal from Dexter."

"Have you been sworn in, sir?"

"Aw, that's all right now. No more rag chewin' out of you. That'll do YOU! Keep your hands up!"

"What am I charged with?"

"Attempted horse stealin', an' you know it."

"Have you a warrant? What is my name?"

"That'll do you now; that'll do you."

"See here, my fine friend, you've made a sad mistake. I'm not the man you want. I'm ready to go to jail, if you insist, but it cost you every dollar you have in the world. I'll make you pay dearly for calling an honest man a thief, sir." Crosby's indignation was beautifully assumed and it took effect.

"Mr. Austin is the man who ordered your arrest," he explained. "I know Mrs. Delancy here all right, an' she left Austin's with you."

"What are you talking about, man? She is my cousin and drove over here this evening to see me between trains. I think you'd better lower your gun, my friend. This will go mighty hard with you."

"But---"

"He has you confused with that horse thief who said his name was Crosby, Tom," said she, pinching his arm delightedly. "He was the worst-looking brute I ever saw. I thought Mr. Austin had him so secure with the bulldog as guardian. Did he escape?"

"Yes, an' you went with him," exclaimed Brown, making a final stand. "An' I know all about how you come over here in Scott Higgins's wagon too."

"The man is crazy!" exclaimed Mrs. Delancy.

"He may have escaped from the asylum up north of here," whispered Crosby, loud enough for the deputy to hear.

"Here comes the train," cried she. "Now we can ask the train men to disarm him and send him back to the asylum. Isn't it awful that such dangerous people can be at large?"

Brown lowered his pistol as the engine thundered past. The pilot was almost in the long bridge at the end of the depot when the train stopped to wait for the eastbound express to pass. The instant that Brown's revolver arm was lowered and his head turned with uncertainty to look at the train, Crosby's hand went to his coat pocket, and when the deputy turned toward him again he found himself looking into the shiny, glittering barrel of a pistol.

"Throw that gun away, my friend," said Crosby in a low tone, "or I'll blow your brains out."

"Great Scott!" gasped Brown.

"Throw it away!"

"Don't kill him," pleaded Mrs. Delancy. Brown's knees were shaking like leaves and his teeth chattered. His revolver sailed through the air and clattered on the brick pavement beyond the end of the platform. "Don't shoot," he pleaded, ready to drop to his knees.

"I won't if you are good and kind and obliging," said Crosby sternly. "Turn around--face the engine. That's right. Now listen to me. I've got this pistol jammed squarely against your back, and if you make a false move--well, you won't have time to regret it. Answer my questions too. How long is that bridge?"

"I--I do--don't kno--ow."

"It's rather long, isn't it?"

"With the fill and trestle it's nearly half a mile."

"What is the next stop west of here for this train?"

"Hopville, forty mile west."

"Where does the east-bound train stop next after leaving here?"

"It don't stop till it gits over in Indiana, thirty mile or more."

"I'm much obliged to you. Now walk straight ahead until you come to the blind end of the mail car."

At the front end of the mail car Crosby and his prisoner halted. Every one knows that the head end of the coach just back of the engine tender is "blind." That is, there is no door leading to the interior, and one must stand outside on the narrow platform if, perchance, he is there when the train starts. As the east-bound train pulled in from the bridge, coming to a stop on the track beyond the west-bound train, Crosby commanded his erstwhile captor to climb aboard the blind end of the mail coach.

"Geewhillikers, don't make me do that," groaned the unhappy Brown.

"Get aboard and don't argue. You can come back to-morrow, you know, and you're perfectly safe if you stay awake and don't roll off. Hurry up! If you try to jump off before you reach the bridge I'll shoot."

A moment later the train pulled into the bridge and Crosby hurried back to his anxious companion. Brown was on his way to a station forty miles west, and he did not dare risk jumping off. By the time the train reached the far end of the bridge it was running forty miles an hour.

"Where is he?" she cried in alarm as he rushed with her across the intervening space to the coveted "east-bound."

"I'll tell you all about it when we get inside this train," he answered. "I think Brown is where he can't telegraph to head us off any place along the line, and if we once get into Indiana we are comparatively safe. Up you go!" and he lifted her up the car steps.

"Safe," she sighed, as they dropped into a seat in a coach.

"I'm ashamed to mention it, my dear accomplice, but are you quite sure you have your purse with you? With the usual luck of a common thief, I am penniless."

"Penniless because you gave your fortune to the cause of freedom," she supplemented, fumbling in her chatelaine bag for her purse. "Here it is. The contents are yours until the end of our romance."

The conductor took fare from him to Lafayette and informed the mud- covered gentleman that he could get a train from that city to Chicago at 2:30 in the morning.

"We're all right now," said Crosby after the conductor had passed on. "You are tired, little woman. Lie back and go to sleep. The rough part of the adventure is almost over." He secured a pillow for her, and she was soon resting as comfortably as it was possible in the day coach of a passenger train.

For many minutes he sat beside her, his eyes resting on the beautiful tired face with its closed eyes, long lashes, pensive mouth, and its frame of dark hair, disarranged and wild.

"It's strange," he thought, almost aloud, "how suddenly it comes to a fellow. Twelve hours ago I was as free as a bird in the air, and now--"

Just then her eyes opened widely with a start, as if she had suddenly come from a rather terrifying dream. They looked squarely into his, and he felt so abashed that he was about to turn away when, with a little catch in her voice, she exclaimed:

"Good heavens!"

"What is it?" he cried.

"You are not married, are you?"

"NO!!!"

Like a culprit caught she blushed furiously, and her eyes wavered as the lids fell, shutting from his eager, surprised gaze the prettiest confusion in the world.

"I--It just occurred to me to ask," she murmured.

Crosby's exhilaration was so great that, after a long, hungry look at the peaceful face, he jumped up and went out into the vestibule, where he whistled with all the ardor of a school-boy. When he returned to his seat beside her she was awake, and the little look of distress left her face when he appeared, a happy smile succeeding.

"I thought you had deserted me," she said.

"Perish the thought."

"Mr. Crosby, if you had a pistol all the time we were in the barn, why did you not shoot the dog and free us hours before you did?" she asked sternly.

"I had no pistol," he grinned. From his pocket he drew a nickel-plated menthol inhaler and calmly leveled it at her head. "It looked very much like a pistol in the darkness," he said, "and it deserves a place among the cherished relics descending from our romance."

The next night two happy, contented persons sat in a brilliant Chicago theatre, and there was nothing in their appearance to indicate that the day and night before had been the most strenuous in their lives.

"This is more comfortable than a cross beam in a barn," she smiled.

"But it is more public," he responded.

Three months later--but Crosby won both suits.

The Codes Of Hammurabi And Moses
W. W. Davies

QTY

The discovery of the Hammurabi Code is one of the greatest achievements of archaeology, and is of paramount interest, not only to the student of the Bible, but also to all those interested in ancient history...

Religion   **ISBN:** *1-59462-338-4*   **Pages:132**

MSRP $12.95

The Theory of Moral Sentiments
Adam Smith

QTY

This work from 1749. contains original theories of conscience amd moral judgment and it is the foundation for systemof morals.

Philosophy **ISBN:** *1-59462-777-0*   **Pages:536**

MSRP $19.95

Jessica's First Prayer
Hesba Stretton

QTY

In a screened and secluded corner of one of the many railway-bridges which span the streets of London there could be seen a few years ago, from five o'clock every morning until half past eight, a tidily set-out coffee-stall, consisting of a trestle and board, upon which stood two large tin cans, with a small fire of charcoal burning under each so as to keep the coffee boiling during the early hours of the morning when the work-people were thronging into the city on their way to their daily toil...

Pages:84

Childrens   **ISBN:** *1-59462-373-2*   *MSRP $9.95*

My Life and Work
Henry Ford

QTY

Henry Ford revolutionized the world with his implementation of mass production for the Model T automobile. Gain valuable business insight into his life and work with his own auto-biography... "We have only started on our development of our country we have not as yet, with all our talk of wonderful progress, done more than scratch the surface. The progress has been wonderful enough but..."

Pages:300

Biographies/   **ISBN:** *1-59462-198-5*   *MSRP $21.95* www.bookjungle.com *email: sales@bookjungle.com fax: 630-214-0564 mail: Book Jungle PO Box 2226 Champaign, IL 61825*

The Art of Cross-Examination
Francis Wellman

QTY

I presume it is the experience of every author, after his first book is published upon an important subject, to be almost overwhelmed with a wealth of ideas and illustrations which could readily have been included in his book, and which to his own mind, at least, seem to make a second edition inevitable. Such certainly was the case with me; and when the first edition had reached its sixth impression in five months, I rejoiced to learn that it seemed to my publishers that the book had met with a sufficiently favorable reception to justify a second and considerably enlarged edition. ..

Pages:412

Reference   ISBN: *1-59462-647-2*   *MSRP $19.95*

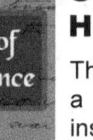

On the Duty of Civil Disobedience
Henry David Thoreau

QTY

Thoreau wrote his famous essay, On the Duty of Civil Disobedience, as a protest against an unjust but popular war and the immoral but popular institution of slave-owning. He did more than write—he declined to pay his taxes, and was hauled off to gaol in consequence. Who can say how much this refusal of his hastened the end of the war and of slavery ?

Law   ISBN: *1-59462-747-9*   **Pages:48**
MSRP $7.45

Dream Psychology Psychoanalysis for Beginners
Sigmund Freud

QTY

Sigmund Freud, born Sigismund Schlomo Freud (May 6, 1856 - September 23, 1939), was a Jewish-Austrian neurologist and psychiatrist who co-founded the psychoanalytic school of psychology. Freud is best known for his theories of the unconscious mind, especially involving the mechanism of repression; his redefinition of sexual desire as mobile and directed towards a wide variety of objects; and his therapeutic techniques, especially his understanding of transference in the therapeutic relationship and the presumed value of dreams as sources of insight into unconscious desires.

Pages:196

Psychology   ISBN: *1-59462-905-6*   *MSRP $15.45*

The Miracle of Right Thought
Orison Swett Marden

QTY

Believe with all of your heart that you will do what you were made to do. When the mind has once formed the habit of holding cheerful, happy, prosperous pictures, it will not be easy to form the opposite habit. It does not matter how improbable or how far away this realization may see, or how dark the prospects may be, if we visualize them as best we can, as vividly as possible, hold tenaciously to them and vigorously struggle to attain them, they will gradually become actualized, realized in the life. But a desire, a longing without endeavor, a yearning abandoned or held indifferently will vanish without realization.

Pages:360

Self Help   ISBN: *1-59462-644-8*   *MSRP $25.45*

www.bookjungle.com *email: sales@bookjungle.com fax: 630-214-0564 mail: Book Jungle PO Box 2226 Champaign, IL 61825*

QTY

The Rosicrucian Cosmo-Conception Mystic Christianity *by **Max Heindel*** ISBN: *1-59462-188-8* **$38.95**
The Rosicrucian Cosmo-conception is not dogmatic, neither does it appeal to any other authority than the reason of the student. It is: not controversial, but is: sent forth in the, hope that it may help to clear.. New Age/Religion Pages 646

Abandonment To Divine Providence *by **Jean-Pierre de Caussade*** ISBN: *1-59462-228-0* **$25.95**
"The Rev. Jean Pierre de Caussade was one of the most remarkable spiritual writers of the Society of Jesus in France in the 18th Century. His death took place at Toulouse in 1751. His works have gone through many editions and have been republished... Inspirational/Religion Pages 400

Mental Chemistry *by **Charles Haanel*** ISBN: *1-59462-192-6* **$23.95**
Mental Chemistry allows the change of material conditions by combining and appropriately utilizing the power of the mind. Much like applied chemistry creates something new and unique out of careful combinations of chemicals the mastery of mental chemistry... New Age Pages 354

The Letters of Robert Browning and Elizabeth Barret Barrett 1845-1846 vol II ISBN: *1-59462-193-4* **$35.95**
*by **Robert Browning** and **Elizabeth Barrett*** Biographies Pages 596

Gleanings In Genesis (volume I) *by **Arthur W. Pink*** ISBN: *1-59462-130-6* **$27.45**
Appropriately has Genesis been termed "the seed plot of the Bible" for in it we have, in germ form, almost all of the great doctrines which are afterwards fully developed in the books of Scripture which follow... Religion/Inspirational Pages 420

The Master Key *by **L. W. de Laurence*** ISBN: *1-59462-001-6* **$30.95**
In no branch of human knowledge has there been a more lively increase of the spirit of research during the past few years than in the study of Psychology, Concentration and Mental Discipline. The requests for authentic lessons in Thought Control, Mental Discipline and... New Age/Business Pages 422

The Lesser Key Of Solomon Goetia *by **L. W. de Laurence*** ISBN: *1-59462-092-X* **$9.95**
This translation of the first book of the "Lernegton" which is now for the first time made accessible to students of Talismanic Magic was done, after careful collation and edition, from numerous Ancient Manuscripts in Hebrew, Latin, and French... New Age/Occult Pages 92

Rubaiyat Of Omar Khayyam *by **Edward Fitzgerald*** ISBN: *1-59462-332-5* **$13.95**
Edward Fitzgerald, whom the world has already learned, in spite of his own efforts to remain within the shadow of anonymity, to look upon as one of the rarest poets of the century, was born at Bredfield, in Suffolk, on the 31st of March, 1809. He was the third son of John Purcell... Music Pages 172

Ancient Law *by **Henry Maine*** ISBN: *1-59462-128-4* **$29.95**
The chief object of the following pages is to indicate some of the earliest ideas of mankind, as they are reflected in Ancient Law, and to point out the relation of those ideas to modern thought. Religion/History Pages 452

Far-Away Stories *by **William J. Locke*** ISBN: *1-59462-129-2* **$19.45**
"Good wine needs no bush, but a collection of mixed vintages does. And this book is just such a collection. Some of the stories I do not want to remain buried for ever in the museum files of dead magazine-numbers an author's not unpardonable vanity..." Fiction Pages 272

Life of David Crockett *by **David Crockett*** ISBN: *1-59462-250-7* **$27.45**
"Colonel David Crockett was one of the most remarkable men of the times in which he lived. Born in humble life, but gifted with a strong will, an indomitable courage, and unremitting perseverance... Biographies/New Age Pages 424

Lip-Reading *by **Edward Nitchie*** ISBN: *1-59462-206-X* **$25.95**
Edward B. Nitchie, founder of the New York School for the Hard of Hearing, now the Nitchie School of Lip-Reading, Inc, wrote "LIP-READING Principles and Practice". The development and perfecting of this meritorious work on lip-reading was an undertaking... How-to Pages 400

A Handbook of Suggestive Therapeutics, Applied Hypnotism, Psychic Science ISBN: *1-59462-214-0* **$24.95**
*by **Henry Munro*** Health/New Age/Health/Self-help Pages 376

A Doll's House: and Two Other Plays *by **Henrik Ibsen*** ISBN: *1-59462-112-8* **$19.95**
Henrik Ibsen created this classic when in revolutionary 1848 Rome. Introducing some striking concepts in playwriting for the realist genre, this play has been studied the world over. Fiction/Classics/Plays 308

The Light of Asia *by **sir Edwin Arnold*** ISBN: *1-59462-204-3* **$13.95**
In this poetic masterpiece, Edwin Arnold describes the life and teachings of Buddha. The man who was to become known as Buddha to the world was born as Prince Gautama of India but he rejected the worldly riches and abandoned the reigns of power when... Religion/History/Biographies Pages 170

The Complete Works of Guy de Maupassant *by **Guy de Maupassant*** ISBN: *1-59462-157-8* **$16.95**
"For days and days, nights and nights, I had dreamed of that first kiss which was to consecrate our engagement, and I knew not on what spot I should put my lips..." Fiction/Classics Pages 240

The Art of Cross-Examination *by **Francis L. Wellman*** ISBN: *1-59462-309-0* **$26.95**
Written by a renowned trial lawyer, Wellman imparts his experience and uses case studies to explain how to use psychology to extract desired information through questioning. How-to/Science/Reference Pages 408

Answered or Unanswered? *by **Louisa Vaughan*** ISBN: *1-59462-248-5* **$10.95**
Miracles of Faith in China Religion Pages 112

The Edinburgh Lectures on Mental Science (1909) *by **Thomas*** ISBN: *1-59462-008-3* **$11.95**
This book contains the substance of a course of lectures recently given by the writer in the Queen Street Hall, Edinburgh. Its purpose is to indicate the Natural Principles governing the relation between Mental Action and Material Conditions... New Age/Psychology Pages 148

Ayesha *by **H. Rider Haggard*** ISBN: *1-59462-301-5* **$24.95**
Verily and indeed it is the unexpected that happens! Probably if there was one person upon the earth from whom the Editor of this, and of a certain previous history, did not expect to hear again... Classics Pages 380

Ayala's Angel *by **Anthony Trollope*** ISBN: *1-59462-352-X* **$29.95**
The two girls were both pretty, but Lucy who was twenty-one who supposed to be simple and comparatively unattractive, whereas Ayala was credited, as her Bombwhat romantic name might show, with poetic charm and a taste for romance. Ayala when her father died was nineteen... Fiction Pages 484

The American Commonwealth *by **James Bryce*** ISBN: *1-59462-286-8* **$34.45**
An interpretation of American democratic political theory. It examines political mechanics and society from the perspective of Scotsman James Bryce Politics Pages 572

Stories of the Pilgrims *by **Margaret P. Pumphrey*** ISBN: *1-59462-116-0* **$17.95**
This book explores pilgrims religious oppression in England as well as their escape to Holland and eventual crossing to America on the Mayflower, and their early days in New England... History Pages 268

www.bookjungle.com *email: sales@bookjungle.com fax: 630-214-0564 mail: Book Jungle PO Box 2226 Champaign, IL 61825*

QTY

The Fasting Cure *by Sinclair Upton*   ISBN: *1-59462-222-1*   **$13.95**
In the Cosmopolitan Magazine for May, 1910, and in the Contemporary Review (London) for April, 1910, I published an article dealing with my experi-
ences in fasting. I have written a great many magazine articles, but never one which attracted so much attention... New Age/Self Help/Health Pages 164

Hebrew Astrology *by Sepharial*   ISBN: *1-59462-308-2*   **$13.45**
In these days of advanced thinking it is a matter of common observation that we have left many of the old landmarks behind and that we are now pressing
forward to greater heights and to a wider horizon than that which represented the mind-content of our progenitors... Astrology Pages 144

Thought Vibration or The Law of Attraction in the Thought World   ISBN: *1-59462-127-6*   **$12.95**

by William Walker Atkinson   Psychology/Religion Pages 144

Optimism *by Helen Keller*   ISBN: *1-59462-108-X*   **$15.95**
Helen Keller was blind, deaf, and mute since 19 months old, yet famously learned how to overcome these handicaps, communicate with the world, and
spread her lectures promoting optimism. An inspiring read for everyone... Biographies/Inspirational Pages 84

Sara Crewe *by Frances Burnett*   ISBN: *1-59462-360-0*   **$9.45**
In the first place, Miss Minchin lived in London. Her home was a large, dull, tall one, in a large, dull square, where all the houses were alike, and all the
sparrows were alike, and where all the door-knockers made the same heavy sound... Childrens/Classic Pages 88

The Autobiography of Benjamin Franklin *by Benjamin Franklin*   ISBN: *1-59462-135-7*   **$24.95**
The Autobiography of Benjamin Franklin has probably been more extensively read than any other American historical work, and no other book of its kind
has had such ups and downs of fortune. Franklin lived for many years in England, where he was agent... Biographies/History Pages 332

Name	
Email	
Telephone	
Address	
City, State ZIP	

☐ **Credit Card**   ☐ **Check / Money Order**

Credit Card Number	
Expiration Date	
Signature	

Please Mail to: Book Jungle
PO Box 2226
Champaign, IL 61825
or Fax to: 630-214-0564

ORDERING INFORMATION

web: *www.bookjungle.com*
email: *sales@bookjungle.com*
fax: *630-214-0564*
mail: *Book Jungle PO Box 2226 Champaign, IL 61825*
or PayPal *to sales@bookjungle.com*

Please contact us for bulk discounts

DIRECT-ORDER TERMS

20% Discount if You Order
Two or More Books
Free Domestic Shipping!
Accepted: Master Card, Visa,
Discover, American Express